The Disappearing Dog Trick

Also by Scott Corbett
The Hangman's Ghost Trick

**Other APPLE® PAPERBACKS
you will want to read:**

Aldo Applesauce
  by Johanna Hurwitz
Arthur, for the Very First Time
  by Patricia MacLachlan
The Chicken Bone Wish
(hardcover title: Joshua, The Czar, and The Chicken Bone Wish)
  by Barbara Girion
Encyclopedia Brown Solves Them All
  by Donald J. Sobol
A Taste of Blackberries
  by Doris Buchanan Smith
Wally
  by Judie Wolkoff

About the Author
A native of Kansas City, Missouri, Scott Corbett
and his wife live in Providence, Rhode Island. He is
the author of many books for children and adults.

The Disappearing Dog Trick

by
Scott Corbett

Illustrated by
Paul Galdone

AN
APPLE®
PAPERBACK

SCHOLASTIC INC.
New York Toronto London Auckland Sydney Tokyo

ISBN 0-590-40973-5

12 11 10 9 8 7 6 5 4 3   6 7 8 9/8 01 2/9

Printed in the U.S.A.   28

With Love
To Tina

1

KERBY MAXWELL and his friend Fenton Claypool were looking forward to a big Saturday night.

They were going to have a weenie roast in the vacant lot and sleep out in the clubhouse, and *nobody* else was going to be around.

Kerby's back yard was separated from the back of the lot by a fence. The house next door to his was separated from it by a hedge. Fenton lived on one side of the lot, and a boy named Bumps Burton lived on the other side.

That Saturday, though, everybody was away, or going to be.

Fenton's parents were away at a conference his father had to attend. Fenton was staying with Kerby while they were gone.

Bumps Burton and his family were away on a vacation trip.

As for Mrs. Pembroke, who lived next door, Kerby had seen her get into a car with some friends. And not only did she take a suitcase, but also her old cat Xerxes in his basket.

And now Kerby's mother and father were invited out to have dinner and play cards, and they had agreed to let Kerby and Fenton stay home alone and have their outing.

It was a very special occasion. There might never be another Saturday night when everybody else would be away at once.

The boys were talking about it as they hurried home along the path through Peterson Park, a small public park where they often played.

"Mom said she wanted us home for final instructions before they left, so we'd better get a move on."

"We'll just make it," said Fenton, consulting his wrist watch.

"Good." Kerby glanced back. "Now where's Waldo gotten to? Here, Waldo! Come on, boy!"

Both boys paused for a look in all directions, and Kerby called several more times, but Waldo did not respond.

"Darn that dog! It's getting so he's always off somewhere on his own!"

"Listen!" cried Fenton. "I hear him!"

The series of short, playful yaps that reached their ears came unmistakably from Waldo. Leaving the path, the boys cut through a small grove of trees in the direction of the sounds.

On the far side of the grove they found Waldo having a

romp with a small black bull terrier named Buster who lived over on Pine Street. He and Waldo were racing around each other in circles, coming to sudden stops with their tails up and their heads down on the ground between their front paws, leaping at each other and grappling in midair, then racing away in circles again.

They were more or less the same size. Waldo was a flop-eared, shaggy combination of several interesting kinds of dog, and he was still about half puppy, even though he was already nearly as big as he was going to get. He obeyed Kerby better all the time now, but he was far from being what you might call trained. And lately he had been venturing off on his own much too often to suit Kerby.

"Waldo!" said his master sternly. Waldo stopped and cocked a brown eye at him, a twinkling brown eye that quickly took on a suitably meek look when he saw that Kerby was really annoyed.

"Now you're going to make us late, with all your fooling around!" Kerby went on. Grabbing the culprit's ear and giving it a smart tug, he pointed sternly homeward. "You come home with us this minute! If you don't watch out, I'll have to start bringing along your *leash!*"

The tug on his ear did not really hurt, but the mention of that dreadful object, his leash, made Waldo wince and utter

5

a few small whining noises. When Kerby released his ear and the boys started running again, back through the trees to the path, Waldo scampered along obediently at their heels, leaving Buster to sit and watch them go.

2

THE BOYS had just passed the drinking fountain, which always made Kerby think of Mrs. Graymalkin, when he looked ahead and thought he saw her. The same droopy hat with the enormous feather trailing from it, the same draggly black cape over a draggly black dress . . .

"Hey! There's Mrs. Graymalkin!"

"Where?"

"She just went around the turn up ahead! Come on!"

They raced as hard as they could to the bend. But when they reached it, the path ahead was empty. Nobody was in sight. Nothing moved among the long tree-shadows that faded as the setting sun sank behind a dark cloud. Kerby rubbed his eyes and stared around.

"I could have sworn I saw her!"

"I wish you had, Kerby. I'd certainly like to see her for myself."

Fenton had never seen Mrs. Graymalkin, but Kerby had told him all about his meetings with her. First Kerby had helped her when the heel of her shoe was caught in the drain by the drinking fountain. Then she had brought him a present as a reward for helping her.

She had brought him an old chemistry set that had once belonged to her own son. And that, of course, had led to all sorts of strange adventures for both of them, Kerby and Fenton — and Waldo, too, for that matter. So naturally Fenton was interested in seeing Mrs. Graymalkin for himself.

"It was just about this time of night when I met her that first time," said Kerby. "Well, come on, let's go, or my folks will be sore."

Soon they were out of the park and running along Kerby's block. Waldo rushed on ahead, looking eagerly for any sign of Xerxes. Usually at about that time of day Xerxes would be hanging around out in front, waiting for Waldo to chase him up a tree. Xerxes enjoyed showing off how good he was at climbing trees. He also enjoyed spitting at Waldo from an overhanging limb. And as for Waldo, few things gave him more pleasure than to stand up against a tree trunk and bark importantly at Xerxes.

"I can't get it through that dog's head that Xerxes is away for the weekend," grumbled Kerby, and yelled to Waldo that he was wasting his time.

Since Mrs. Pembroke was away, they treated themselves

to the luxury of a short-cut gallop across her lawn, and raced between the houses and up the back steps and into Kerby's house.

Kerby's mother was standing in the middle of the kitchen, tapping her foot. She was all dressed up and had a hat on.

"You're late." She glanced around at Kerby's father, who appeared just then. "I'm not sure we should leave these two alone, if they can't follow orders any better than this."

"Aw gee, Mom, we're only about two minutes late!"

"Well, that's two too many. I want you where I tell you to be *when* I tell you to be there, especially when we're going out."

Kerby's father had been glancing at the front page of the evening newspaper. He tossed it aside and looked at the boys solemnly.

"Pris, I still think we should have gotten a baby sitter."

Fenton spoke up in his polite way, but with a twinkle in his eye.

"Oh, you don't have to spend any money for a baby sitter, Mr. Maxwell — I'm glad to sit with Kerby for nothing."

"Oh, you funnyman!" cried Kerby, and began a scuffle which they broke off as quickly as they began it — and both of them cried, "Not in the house!" a split second before Mrs.

Maxwell managed to say it. This made her giggle and shake her head helplessly.

"Really, what am I going to do with you two? Now, pay attention to me, because we have to leave. You have all your food?"

"Yes, Mom. Everything's in the cooler out in the clubhouse."

"Your sleeping bags are out there?"

"Yes, Mom."

"Lock the back door when you leave and put the key in the garage."

"Yes, Mom."

"We won't be later than ten-thirty getting home, and when we do we'll come out to see if everything's all right."

"Gee, do you have to, Mom?"

"Don't worry, we won't spoil anything, because you won't even know about it. You'll be asleep by then. At least, you'd better be," she added, with a stern glance at each of them.

"Okay, Mom."

Mr. Maxwell held up a small circle of shiny metal.

"Why hasn't this been put on Waldo's collar?"

"Well, gee, Dad, I've been meaning to put it on."

"Well, do it. I don't want Waldo to set a paw out of this

house again until he's wearing it. See what it says right here in the paper?" He pointed to a story on the front page. "Any dogs found not wearing their new license tags are going to be picked up. There's a real drive on. All the city trucks are out, and they mean business. So take care of that, because I don't want to have to chase over to the city dog pound looking for Waldo."

"Yes, Pop. I'll put it on right away."

"You do that. Well, have a good weenie roast. Remember, we're at the Barretts' and their telephone number is on the pad by the telephone, if you want us for anything."

"Okay, Pop."

Mrs. Maxwell turned back at the front door with a mother's typical worried look.

"We may get a storm tonight. If it starts storming, I want you three to march straight into the house, do you hear?"

"Okay, Mom," sighed Kerby. He knew it was no use arguing. A few drops of rain never hurt anyone, and anyway the clubhouse didn't leak very much at all, but try to tell that to your mother!

The three of them stood at a window, Waldo with his front paws up on the sill, watching Kerby's parents drive away.

"Why is it they always tell you to *march* when it's something you don't want to do?" Kerby wondered. "It's always

12

'March in and wash your face' or 'March right upstairs and write those thank-you letters.' They never say, 'March in here and eat some ice cream' or 'March outside and play ball.'"

Fenton agreed it was a funny thing, and said it was enough to make a fellow hate marching. Kerby felt something in his hand, and remembered he was holding the dog tag.

"Come on, let's put this on Waldo's collar, so we can go out and get our fire going and start roasting some weenies. I'm hungry!"

Waldo had moved over to a side window and was looking out at Mrs. Pembroke's yard.

"Look, Waldo, I *told* you, Xerxes has gone away for the weekend," said Kerby as he unfastened Waldo's collar, but Waldo did not even get down from the window. He was a hard dog to convince.

They took the collar down to the basement workbench. Fenton held it while Kerby pried open the ring with the old tag on it.

"I sure wish that *had* been Mrs Graymalkin I saw," said Kerby while they worked. "I'd like to tell her about what happened when we used that chemistry set she gave me. I'd like to hear what she'd have to say about *that!*"

"She said it belonged to her son Felix when he was a little

14

boy, didn't she? Well, I wonder if she fooled him into using some of that stuff we used for the lemonade trick whenever she wanted him to be specially good?"

They discussed this interesting question until they had the new dog tag in place, dangling from the ring. Then they took the collar upstairs.

"Come here, Waldo," said Kerby, walking into the living room. But Waldo was not there.

"I guess he finally gave up on Xerxes," said Fenton.

"Probably he's upstairs," said Kerby, and went to the foot of the stairs to call up to the second floor. "Hey, Waldo, come down here!"

But no sound of toenails clicking on the upstairs hall floor answered his call. As they listened, the house was very quiet. Too quiet.

"I'll bet he's sneaked onto one of the beds and is keeping still about it," said Kerby. He went upstairs to find Waldo and give him a lecture.

But Waldo was not on any of the beds, nor in any of the closets, nor even under any of the beds. When Kerby came back down, he was concerned. And he found Fenton looking concerned, too.

"Come to think of it, I heard the screen door bump, the

way it does when he pushes his way out with his nose," said Fenton, "but we were busy talking, and I didn't really stop to think about it at the time."

"Come to think of it, I heard something, too," said Kerby. "That crazy dog! He wasn't supposed to go outside again without his new tag on, and now he's gone without even a collar on! We've got to get him right back in here!"

They hurried outside, calling anxiously. But Waldo was not in the back yard, nor was he in the front yard. Nor was he over in Mrs. Pembroke's yard where he knew he should never, never go, but often went.

"Maybe he went out to the clubhouse," suggested Fenton. Waldo sometimes did that. They returned to the back yard, pushed the loose board in the fence aside and slipped through, and ran out to the clubhouse, calling Waldo, and whistling for him as loud as they could.

The clubhouse was about the size of a big packing crate. They had built it themselves out of old boards, and except for a tendency to lean it was a fine clubhouse. In front of it was a circle of stones, where they built their campfires and where they had planned to roast their weenies that very night.

"Waldo! Waldo!" called Kerby, and even looked inside the clubhouse. But Waldo was nowhere to be found.

Now Kerby was really worried. He could picture a dogcatcher's truck pulling up, and a man with a net swooping down on poor Waldo and scooping him up and taking him off to the city dog pound. He could picture his father's face when he heard the news.

"I'll bet Waldo went back over to the park," he said, and Fenton agreed. Kerby turned and started running. "Come on, then — let's hurry!"

3

"YOU take the path, and I'll take the wall," suggested Fenton. "That way we can cover the whole park better."

"Okay," said Kerby, and they split up to search for Waldo.

A dusky haze hung over the park now. Kerby's heart sank as he thought of how soon it would be dark. They had to find Waldo in a hurry, or they might not find him at all.

The park was nearly deserted. Kerby did not see a soul all the way to the drinking fountain. Then, as he rounded the bend, remembering that this was the very spot where he had thought he saw Mrs. Graymalkin less than an hour ago — he saw her again.

This time there was no mistake about it. She was walking straight toward him. When he shouted "Mrs. Graymalkin!" she stopped and watched him run to her.

She smiled, and it looked to Kerby as if there were just as many gaps between her teeth as ever, if not more. Her squashy hat with the enormous feather drooping down from it looked the same. So did her draggly old black cape and dress. So did the high-heeled shoes that seemed so strange on such an old lady.

"Why, Kerby!" she cackled, as pleased as could be. "I haven't seen you for a long time! Where have you been?"

"Where have *you* been?" said Kerby. "I've looked all over for you, lots of times!"

"Well, I'm sorry we missed each other. But what are you doing here at this hour, running in the wrong direction? Shouldn't you be on your way home?"

"Waldo's missing! He sneaked out of the house without his collar on, and if I don't find him he's liable to be picked up by the dogcatcher!"

"Waldo? That dear little dog of yours? How is he?"

"Well, he *was* fine, but —"

"You say he's missing?"

"Yes! Are you sure you haven't seen him around here, Mrs. Graymalkin?"

"Waldo, Waldo . . . No, I haven't seen him, I'm afraid, but I certainly must help you find him if I can. After all, you were so nice to me . . ."

"Aw, shucks." Kerby reddened modestly. "I only helped you a little bit . . ."

"Well, you were a very nice boy, and I'd like to help *you* now if I can."

Mrs. Graymalkin rolled her eyes up, frowned prodigiously, and put a finger alongside her wrinkled lips.

"Tell me, Kerby, do you still have that chemistry set I gave you?"

"Oh, sure! I've got it hid —"

Kerby stopped, and turned red all over again. Mrs. Graymalkin's bright sharp eyes peered down at him all a-twinkle.

"Hid?"

"Well, after what went on when I tried that trick you told me about," said Kerby, sort of accusingly, "I didn't want to have to explain about the chemistry set to my mother and father. So I put it in my chest in the basement that I keep old toys in. I hid it under all my old blocks. Besides, nobody ever opens my chest but me."

"I see. Well, perhaps you were wise. Not everybody would understand about our 'Feats O' Magic' chemistry set, not even nice parents such as I'm sure you have. But at any rate, it might be that one of my son Felix's favorite feats of magic could help you find Waldo."

"Honest? Gee, I hope so!"

"Well, I certainly hope so, too. Now, I'll tell you what to do. Use the . . . let me see . . ."

Mrs. Graymalkin squeezed her eyes shut for a moment and laid her bony finger alongside her nose. Kerby decided it must

be her thinking finger, because she always seemed to put it alongside her nose or her lips when she was trying hard to think about something.

Her eyes popped open.

"I have it! The second tube from the right! Remember that, now — the second tube from the right! Drop nine drops into a beaker — three times three, thrice thrice. Then wait a moment. It will begin to bubble and boil and steam —"

"You said that the last time," Kerby reminded her, "but it didn't do it! It did plenty else, but it didn't bubble and boil and steam!"

"Never mind last time, this is *this* time!" retorted Mrs. Graymalkin with a cackle. "Do as I tell you, and then think about Waldo and —"

"Kerby!"

From somewhere in the distance came Fenton's anxious call. Kerby glanced past Mrs. Graymalkin, but could not see him.

"That's my friend Fenton. Hey, Fenton!"

"Run and fetch him," said Mrs. Graymalkin. "I'd like to meet him."

Kerby raced down the path, saw Fenton coming, and signaled frantically.

"Come on! Mrs. Graymalkin is here!"

Fenton broke his stride. In fact, he nearly fell over his own feet. But once he had recovered, he sprinted like a track star. Together they ran back to see Mrs. Graymalkin.

She was gone.

The shadows under the thick trees of the park were deep now, and the boys were alone. They looked at each other. Fenton did not even seem very surprised.

"I don't understand," said Kerby. "She said she wanted to meet you, and she sent me to fetch you."

"I'm afraid you're the only one she really wants to see," said Fenton sadly.

"Well, just the same, she was right here, and I told her about Waldo, and she told me about a trick with the chemistry set she said might help us find him!"

Fenton grabbed his arm.

"Did she? Well, let's go, then! Let's go home and try it! Because I looked all over, and Waldo isn't in the park anywhere!"

Kerby carefully lifted the long box out of his toy chest and carried it to the workbench.

The outside of the box was plain, but when he opened it the inside of the lid was covered with printing in faded red and black letters:

FEATS O' MAGIC CHEMISTRY SET

Instructive! Entertaining!
Hours of Amusement!
Astonish Your Friends!
Entertain at Parties!
Make Extra Money Giving Demonstrations!

Lying in a row were corked glass tubes with various amounts of liquids in them. Each had a faded label on it. One slot was empty, of course — the one that had contained the tube they used to do the lemonade trick. But all the other tubes were still there.

A separate section of the box was full of eyedroppers, retorts, special tubes, and glass containers called beakers.

"The second tube from the right, she said."

Kerby held it up.

"Not much left in it," he grumbled. "She always seems to pick the ones her son Felix used the most of."

"We'll be lucky to get nine drops out of that," said Fenton.

Kerby uncorked the tube and sniffed it cautiously.

"Phew! Chemicals mostly smell bad, don't they?"

Fenton sniffed.

"Hmm. This one does, anyway. Here, better use this eyedropper. Its rubber end still seems to be okay, and besides, it's the longest."

But even the longest eyedropper could not quite reach the small amount of liquid left in the tube.

"Tell you what, Kerby, why not pour it into a beaker first, and then you can get at it with the eyedropper. All you'll have to do is pull it all into the eyedropper and then drop nine drops back into the beaker."

"Good idea."

Kerby set a beaker out on the workbench. He poured the liquid into it and picked up the long eyedropper. Then he hesitated.

"Say, why not save this big one for something else? I can get at the stuff with a short one now."

They were looking over the various eyedroppers, trying to decide which one to use, when a hissing noise made them jump back.

"What's that?"

The liquid in the beaker was bubbling and boiling and steaming.

A cloudy gas was forming above it.

All at once it went —

POUF!

Like a cloud cannonball from a glass cannon, a round ball of silvery gas puffed out of the beaker and went spinning straight up in the air.

For a moment they stared wordlessly with eyes as round as the gas ball itself, watching it rise and smash silently against the ceiling.

Fenton managed to speak first, but he did not sound natural. His voice had a squeak in it.

"Must have been nine drops, all right!"

"I sure guess it must have!" Kerby craned his neck forward cautiously. "Something's happened to the beaker! I can't see through it any more!"

They stared at each other, wondering if they dared go closer. The beaker was silent.

"I guess it's through popping off," decided Fenton.

"Let's look at it."

Gingerly they edged forward and looked into it.

"Why, it's like a mirror inside now!" marveled Kerby.

"Yes, but I can't see myself, can you?"

"No . . ."

"I can't see anything, except . . ."

"Except what, Fenton?"

"Well, except a funny sort of optical illusion."

"What's an optical illusion?"

26

Fenton knew lots of big words. He was not at the head of their class in school for nothing. But somehow his classmates never minded, because Fenton never made the rest of them feel small about it. He just *knew* things.

"Well, that's when you seem to see something that isn't really there," he explained, "or when something looks different than it really is. When something plays tricks on your eyes. The way it looks to me in the beaker, it's as if a glass screen was suspended across the middle of it. Almost like a tiny television screen."

"That's right! That's how it looks to me, too. Say! Mrs. Graymalkin said to think about Waldo."

"Oh, that's so. Let's think about Waldo."

"Hey!"

They stared at each other, pop-eyed again.

"Did you see something?"

"Yes! Did you?"

"Yes!"

"What did you see?"

"Waldo!"

Fenton nodded, his mouth tight with excitement.

"So did I!"

4

THEY LOOKED into the beaker again.

"It's him, all right!"

"And there's Buster!"

"Sure! He's over at Buster's!"

They could see the two dogs sitting side by side on the terraced lawn in front of Buster's house over on Pine Street, watching the cars go by. Kerby and Fenton laughed with relief.

"Why didn't we think of that? Might have known that's where he was when he wasn't in the park! Let's go!"

They hurried up the steps and out the back door.

"We can cut through the lot."

They pushed aside the loose board in the fence, squeezed through, and ran across the vacant lot.

"Mrs. Graymalkin really came through this time, didn't she?" exulted Kerby. "That old chemistry set is great!"

"Terrific!"

"Boy, am I hungry!" Kerby added as they passed their

clubhouse. "Soon as we grab Waldo and put his collar on, let's get a fire started and cook some weenies! I can hardly wait!"

Buster's house was only three blocks away. When they turned the corner onto Pine Street and looked down the block, however, they were jolted to a stop by what they saw.

Buster was standing up on his lawn, barking at a small truck with wire mesh sides that was pulled up at the curb. About twenty dogs of all sizes were inside the wire cage, barking back.

30

One of the smallest and barkingest of these twenty dogs was Waldo.

Before the boys could do more than gasp, the truck began to drive away.

"Hey! Stop!"

Yelling frantically, the boys raced after the truck. But it picked up speed and rattled away down the street before they could even begin to catch up with it. Barking and yelping and yapping and howling, Waldo and his fellow prisoners disappeared into the dusk-filled distant reaches of Pine Street.

The boys sagged to a stop. They watched until they could see the truck no longer. With hot tears trembling in his eyes, Kerby turned his stricken face toward Fenton and saw a face almost as woebegone as his own.

"They got him! Now they'll take him to the dog pound! Golly, what'll my father say?"

Fenton gulped.

"I don't know, Kerby. I guess we're in for it."

Kerby took no time at all to make up his mind about what he was going to do.

"Well, I don't care, I'm going home and call my father right away. I don't want anything to happen to Waldo, no matter what happens to *me!*" he said — though he could not help adding in a gloomy voice, "And plenty will!"

They ran home as fast as they could. Fenton, however, was not letting the time go to waste. As he ran, Fenton was thinking hard.

"Listen, before you call your father let's at least take one more look in the beaker and see how things are going. If we can find out where the city dog pound is, and if that's where they put him, maybe we could take his collar with us and go there. And maybe when they saw you really have a new license tag for Waldo they'd let us take him home."

Naturally, Fenton's idea appealed to Kerby. He was ready to grasp at any straw. Anything. Anything to avoid that awful moment when he would call his father and tell him the news and his father would say, *"What??!"*

And besides that, his mother would get all upset, and along with everything else Kerby thought enough of his parents so that he hated to spoil their evening for them.

But most of all he hated the thought of his father's —
"Wha-a-at???!!!"

It got worse every time he imagined it.

Down at the basement workbench again, they stared once more into the beaker and thought about Waldo.

Nothing happened.

"Come on, come on!"

"Kerby, are you thinking hard?"

"Hard as I can!"

"Well, so am I. Gosh, I hope it's not —"

"There!"

"Yes!"

Slowly, the way scenes sometimes do in a movie, a picture began to appear; fuzzy at first, then gradually becoming sharp and clear.

They were seeing the back end of the truck again.

"Where's Waldo? Do you see him, Fenton?"

"No, not yet. There's so many dogs jumping around . . ."

"There he is!"

Kerby pointed so excitedly that Fenton grabbed his finger.

"Watch out, Kerby! Don't hit the beaker!"

"Oh! Well, anyway, there he is!"

"Yes, I see him now."

"Right behind the little door. Come on, Waldo! Push it open!"

"He can't. See, it's got a peg through the staple to keep it shut. Look! There's the driver, and he's caught another dog in a net."

"Yes, and those people are giving him an argument. They all look mad."

"They sure do. And look at that kid! He's sneaking up to the truck!"

Eagerly both boys bent closer over the beaker as the situation grew more exciting. A tall, slouchy boy a couple of years older than they had edged up to the back of the truck and was reaching for the peg that held the door shut. Grinning wickedly, he paused and peeked around the side of the truck as though to make sure the driver was not looking. His hesitation put Kerby and Fenton into a frenzy of suspense.

"Come on, dopey! Open it!"

"Hurry!"

Still the boy hesitated. He glanced around, this way and that. Kerby clawed the air in agony. It was horrible to watch and be so helpless.

"Please!"

The boy took one last look. Then he reached up and tugged at the peg.

The door swung open, exposing to clearer view the surprised countenance of Waldo, who had been crouched directly behind it. He blinked, and peered cautiously out the open door.

Waldo had never looked less intelligent. By now Kerby and Fenton, watching helplessly, were tearing their hair.

"Don't just stand there!"

"Jump!"

But Waldo just looked, wide-eyed. And then suddenly he disappeared, shouldered aside by a large, mangy Airedale who was in no mood to linger. The Airedale leaped to freedom. Kerby turned away from the beaker, unable to watch any longer, and beat on the wall with his fists. Waldo's golden opportunity, and he had missed it!

"Hey, Kerby!"

At Fenton's cry Kerby leaped back to the beaker as fast as he had left it. Two other dogs had followed the Airedale. And now —

"Look!"

Here came Waldo, skidding stiff-legged toward the door. It was certainly not his idea — he was being pushed. He was simply caught in the rush.

With a wild rolling look in his big brown eyes, he came shooting through the door and off the back end of the truck with all four legs thrust out straight. He looked like a dog who had slid off a ski jump and forgotten to put on his skis.

And at that very instant the picture swiftly faded out.

5

THE BOYS stared at the beaker and then at each other.

Next Fenton turned and stared at the chemistry set.

"That set is so old . . . The chemical must have lost some of its power . . ."

Kerby flung himself down on a stool, where he sat with his elbows on his knees and his fists jammed against his jaws. He felt awful. Hollow-eyed, he stared into space.

"I wish he hadn't jumped! Before, we at least knew where he was, and where he was going. Now we don't even know that!"

"Well, we know the general direction . . ."

"What good is that?"

"Not much, I guess."

For a moment Kerby felt beaten. Then, "Come on, Fenton," he said grimly. "Let's take one more look and think about Waldo harder than we ever thought before."

The way they concentrated this time, it was a wonder the beaker did not split squarely in two.

At first they saw nothing. Gradually, however, a vague, hazy picture appeared . . . cleared . . . sharpened.

"There!"

Waldo was peeking around a garbage can in an alley. The alley was between two red brick walls. Judging from the garbage can (which was badly dented) and the alley (which was dark and dirty) and the walls (which appeared to belong to shabby apartment buildings), Waldo was not in a very good neighborhood.

"Where is he?"

"Who knows?"

"Waldo! Get out of that alley and walk past something!"

"Yes, for crying out loud, Waldo, walk past a street sign so we'll know where you are!"

But Waldo was taking a long, cautious look around. His manner was that of a dog who had recently been chased, and did not care to be chased again if he could help it.

Having satisfied himself that no man with a net was in sight, Waldo edged out of the alley and began trotting along the sidewalk.

"Watch for numbers on windows, store signs — anything!" cried Fenton.

Waldo trotted past a dingy apartment house with the number 104 on one side of its double entrance doors.

"One-oh-four! One-oh-four *what?*" groaned Fenton.

Next to the apartment house was a Chinese laundry. And as Waldo paused and looked in the open door, the picture faded out again.

"Won Ding Lee!" cried Fenton.

"Wong Ling Yee!" cried Kerby.

"I'm sure it was Won Ding Lee!"

"No, it was Wong Ling Yee!"

"Let's look in the phone book!" Fenton raced for the stairs with Kerby hot on his heels.

They found no Chinese laundry listed under Won.

"Wong, then . . . Wong . . . Wong *Ding* Yee!" yelled Fenton.

"Ding?"

"Yes."

"Not Ling?"

"No, Ding."

"Well, maybe it was Ding."

"Ding-a-Ling!" said Fenton, and his solemn face split into one of its rare grins.

"Ding-a-Ling!" cried Kerby, amused in spite of himself at the silly sound of it. But right away he felt ashamed. "Ding-a-ling yourself! What are we laughing about? While we're laughing, Waldo may be in danger! What's the address of Ding-a-Ling's laundry?"

"One-oh-eight Caswell Street."

"Where's that?"

"Search me."

Kerby snapped his fingers.

"My father's got a city street map! It's in the bookcase."

He found the map and they spread it out on the living room floor. On hands and knees they searched for Caswell Street. Soon Fenton's finger jabbed the map.

"Here it is!"

"Why, it's nearly downtown!"

Kerby jumped to his feet. "Well, come on, we've got to go after him!"

From his hands and knees Fenton rocked back into a squatting position and stayed that way, thinking, his eyes glinting as he planned.

"Wait a minute, Kerby. Not so fast. We have to get organized. There's lots of things we need to think of. First of all, how are we going to get down to Caswell Street?"

"Well . . . take a bus, I guess."

"And how are we going to know where to look for Waldo when we *do* get there? We've got to take along the beaker and hope we can get it working again. And we don't want to forget his collar and leash, to put on him the minute we find him. And then how'll we get home?"

"Take another bus?"

Fenton shook his head.

"Remember those signs painted in all the buses? 'No Pets Allowed!' We'll have to bring him home in a taxi."

"A *taxi*?"

"Yes. And that costs a lot of money."

"Well, I should hope to tell you it does!"

"How much have you got, Kerby? I've got a dollar my dad gave me for the weekend."

Kerby felt around in the pockets of his shorts and brought forth a thin dime. He looked at it ruefully, remembering the fifty cents he had squandered on candy and a movie the night before.

"I've only got one measly — wait a minute! I've got a dollar, too! I've got the dollar I made mowing Mrs. Farber's lawn — the one I used to start filling up my new savings bank!"

Kerby sped away upstairs and robbed the bank. While he was there he grabbed a box off his desk and brought that down with him, too.

"Here's the box that special glue came in I sent away for,"

42

he yelled as he came downstairs. "It's got excelsior in it and everything."

Fenton was just hurrying back into the room himself. He had been down to the basement to fetch the collar and leash and the beaker.

"Just the thing!" he agreed. Carefully they put the beaker into the box. "We've got to take special care of this, all right — it's our only chance! Okay, now — money, collar, leash, beaker — anything else we need?"

Kerby paused for a split second to think.

"No, let's go!" he cried, tortured by suspense and impatience as he thought of Waldo wandering around and maybe getting into more trouble. Every second they delayed gave Waldo that much more time to get caught again.

"Okay. Let's go out the back way, then, and lock up."

Kerby put Waldo's collar in his pocket while Fenton stuffed the leash in his. Fenton carried the box with the beaker in it so that Kerby could lock the door.

"We're thinking of everything," Kerby remarked admiringly as he hung the key in its hiding-place in the garage.

"I hope so," said Fenton in a worried voice. "I can't think of anything we've missed, but . . ."

They ran around the side of the house and up the street

toward the corner, where the buses stopped. No bus was in sight. Kerby glanced longingly at the drugstore.

"I'm starved, Fenton. What say we get two candy bars with my dime?"

"Well . . ."

"We'll still have my dollar."

"Well . . . The one thing we've got to be sure to do is keep one dollar for the taxicab."

"Will it cost us that much?"

"Easy. Practically every block costs another nickel when you're riding in a taxi."

"Gosh! I suppose maybe we ought to save the dime, too, then."

But Fenton was not made of iron, either.

"Well, no," he said. "I guess we can spare it . . ."

Back at the bus stop after a hasty visit to the drugstore, they silently wolfed down their tiny candy bars, silently dropped the candy wrappers into the corner tilt-lid trash can, and silently thought about how delicious three or four more of the same candy bars would taste. But neither mentioned the fact to the other.

"Here comes a bus!" said Fenton presently, as one nosed around the corner. "I hope it's the right one."

The driver said the bus went to Caswell Street. They

climbed aboard and took seats in the back corner. Fenton muttered something about sitting back there so they could look in the beaker without other people watching.

"But let's wait till we get closer before we look," Fenton added, and Kerby agreed. They both dreaded trying again, for fear the beaker would stop working altogether.

"That crazy chemistry set! If only it wasn't so old!" grumbled Kerby. He glowered at the box Fenton was carrying. Then the wonder of it struck him anew. He had been so busy worrying about Waldo that he had almost forgotten how eerie a thing it was that they were able to look into a glass beaker and see a picture of what Waldo was doing somewhere else. Suddenly the thought of it made him get goose pimples all over. He found himself speaking about it in what was almost a scared whisper.

"Gee, I wonder about Mrs. Graymalkin. You say she's not a witch, but I don't know," he declared, shaking his head. "I just don't know, Fenton. Witches don't have to be bad, you know. There can be good witches, too. Not very often, I'll admit, but sometimes."

At this Fenton got that scientific look on his face.

"Yes, but I don't believe there are such things as witches, good *or* bad." Firmly he repeated the opinion he had given once before, when they had tried the lemonade trick with

such strange results. "I still think she's just an eccentric."

"Somebody that acts funny, but who isn't nutty, but only odd," said Kerby, remembering Fenton's explanation of the term "eccentric."

"That's right, Kerby. I even think that maybe Mrs. Graymalkin *thinks* she's a witch, and if anybody could be a witch she *would* be — but I don't think there *are* witches. It just wouldn't be scientific to have witches."

"All right, Fenton, but if she isn't a witch, then how do you explain a magic beaker that's like a little television set? And not only that, but one that shows us what we want to see?"

Fenton peered down into Kerby's eyes keenly, and jolted him with a question of his own.

"How do you explain television?"

It was a good question. Kerby could not think of anything to say, because he *couldn't* explain television.

"Go ahead, tell me," Fenton persisted. "How does the picture get in the box?"

"I don't know."

"Well, then! Isn't television like magic, Kerby? We sit down in front of a glass screen in a box and watch somebody doing something — somebody who isn't just a twenty-minute bus ride away, but maybe thousands of miles away!"

Kerby nodded. It was really creepy to think of television in those terms.

"And yet, television isn't magic at all," Fenton went on. "We know how it works. Little electric waves we can't even see are sent out through the air. They wiggle in through the TV set and make a picture on the screen."

Kerby was impressed.

"If you understand *that,* you're better than I am!" he admitted.

"Well, I don't understand it all, but that's the idea. So anyway, that's what electric waves can do. Now, the next thing is this, Kerby. We know that our brains send out electric waves, too. We can even measure them."

"You're kidding!"

"No, I'm not. Every time you think, your brain sends out brain waves."

Kerby marveled over this. He even felt his head.

"I'm surprised it doesn't hurt," he remarked.

Fenton demonstrated the process. He put his fingertips against his own forehead and frowned deeply.

"See? I'm thinking," he announced. "And my brain waves are going out in all directions, and bouncing off buildings and everything."

"Golly! That's quite a stunt," said Kerby in an admiring tone of voice.

"No, it isn't. Anybody can do it," Fenton declared modestly. "In fact, we all *do* do it. Can't help it. Now, if we have those waves, why couldn't they go out and *get* a picture and bounce it back to us, somehow? If conditions were right, that is, and we had something to receive the picture on?"

Kerby thought that one over for a moment.

"Well, I suppose they could," he finally agreed. "But what made that chemical turn our beaker into a receiving set?"

"I don't know," Fenton admitted cheerfully, "but if you gave them a chance, I'll bet the scientists could explain it."

The bus had stopped, waiting for a traffic light to change. In the side seat ahead of the boys, a man turned and tugged at a window, trying to raise it higher. His face was red, and beads of perspiration dappled his brow. "Whew! It's certainly close. Not a breath of air stirring!" he remarked to his wife.

"I think it's going to rain," she said. "Didn't I hear thunder a while ago?"

As if in answer to her question, they all heard a low, distant rumble of thunder.

"I guess you did, all right," said the man. "Well, we could certainly use a shower, but I hope it waits till we get home."

Kerby nudged Fenton worriedly.

"Gee, if it rains we're really out of luck!" he muttered. "My folks aren't far from home, and you know my mother — she'll have to come over and check to see if we're all right!"

Fenton peered out the window.

"Well, I don't think it's going to rain soon, and maybe it won't rain at all. That thunder is pretty far away. Sometimes you get heat lightning for hours and nothing ever comes of it."

Kerby felt better, because he knew that one of the many things Fenton had studied up on was the weather. Fenton often pointed out the clouds and said what kind they were, and what they meant as far as the weather was concerned. And several times his predictions had been exactly right, too.

"Well, I hope you're right, Fenton. And I hope my mother doesn't take that thunder too seriously. Because it would be awful if my parents came home and we weren't . . . Hey, what's the matter?"

Fenton's expression was alarming. If Kerby had not known how empty Fenton's stomach was, he would have thought his friend had eaten something that was not agreeing with him. Fenton had gone sort of green in the face, and was gasping for breath.

"Kerby! We forgot something!"

50

"We what?"

"Before we left the house!"

"What are you talking about? I thought we thought of everything!"

"Well, we didn't! It's my fault!" groaned Fenton. "Kerby, when I went down and got the beaker, I forgot all about putting away the chemistry set. It's spread out all over the workbench!"

Kerby felt as if the bus had jolted over a huge hole. That was the way his insides felt.

"Oh, my gosh!" In his mind he searched wildly for a ray of hope, and found one. "Well, even if they should come home, my father probably wouldn't go down there —"

"Oh, yes, he will! Because I'm almost positive I also forgot to turn out the basement light!"

The bus seemed to hit another, even larger hole. This time there was no ray of hope to be found in the blackness.

"He'll notice the light's on," mumbled Kerby in a daze, "and he'll go down to check on things, and . . ."

Both boys' imaginations were working overtime. They could see themselves *trying* to explain about the chemistry set, but they could not see themselves being successful. Each time Kerby attempted to imagine what would happen, he kept ending up in a psychiatrist's office. If they had to tell the true story about the chemistry set, it would sound like one of the biggest lies ever invented!

"Well, all we can do now is find Waldo and get back home again as fast as we can — and hope we get there first!" declared Kerby, sitting forward on the edge of his seat and wishing the bus would go faster. From then on it seemed to them as if the bus stopped about every four feet. And every time it stopped some old lady was waiting to get on or off, and took about a year doing it. And besides that, there was the beaker to worry about. That darned beaker!

"All I wish is that we had some more chemical to use, instead of having a beaker that acts like it's got a bad tube and needs a serviceman to come fix it!" Kerby glanced uneasily at the box in Fenton's hands. "Want to take a look now, and see if we can see Waldo?"

Fenton stared down just as uneasily at the box.

"Well . . . Well, I'll tell you what. Let's wait till we get to Caswell Street, and then if we don't find him somewhere near Ding-a-Ling's . . ."

"Okay!" Kerby nodded in eager agreement. As anxious as he was to know Waldo's whereabouts, he was glad of any excuse not to put the beaker to the test. Because if they did, and it did not work any more, Waldo might be lost for good!

6

CASWELL STREET at last!

When the driver finally called out "Caswell next!" Fenton thought to go up and tell him what number they were looking for, and he told them in which direction to walk.

The houses they passed were old dingy red brick flats or apartment houses.

"This certainly looks like the right street," remarked Fenton, "and the numbers are going the right way."

Looking ahead hopefully, they both let out a glad cry. About a block ahead they could see a sign hanging over the sidewalk.

The sign read, *Wong Ding Yee Hand Laundry*.

They startled two old ladies by crying "Ding-a-Ling!" and racing past them at a great clip. Coming to a tiptoe stop on the corner, they waited impatiently for a chance to dart across the street, then hurried on to Wong Ding Yee's.

The laundry was closed. Black. Dismal. Deserted.

The dark window looked as gloomy as they felt. They exchanged a bitterly disappointing glance. Being optimists by nature, both boys had had visions of a kindly Chinese laundryman who would let Waldo come into his shop and would take care of him until they got there. Somehow it had never occurred to them that they might find the laundry closed and dark.

They both stared down at the box Fenton was carrying. Kerby drew a deep breath.

"Well, we've got to take a look, that's all."

"Here's hoping."

Opening the lid of the box, they stood under a street light and peered earnestly into the beaker, thinking hard about Waldo.

Without much delay this time, a picture formed!

"There he is!"

"Yes! . . . My gosh, Kerby — that's a police station!"

A small Chinese man in dark clothes and a wide-brimmed black hat was leading Waldo up the steps of a building that Fenton had correctly recognized as a police station. Actually, "leading" is not exactly the word to describe the way Mr. Wong was bringing Waldo into the police station. "Dragging" would be more like it. Waldo had a length of clothesline around his neck, and he was hanging back. Mr. Wong

pleaded with him, and pulled gently but firmly on the line, and they went inside.

"I wish we could *hear* something!" muttered Kerby. He did not like to complain about anything as marvelous as the beaker was, but it *did* have its drawbacks. The lack of sound was certainly one of them.

Still, it was not hard to figure out what was happening. Mr. Wong went up to a policeman sitting at a desk and began talking and pointing to Waldo.

"I'll bet he read in the paper about how dogs with no licenses are going to be picked up. He's turning Waldo in!" declared Fenton.

"That's exactly what he's doing!" agreed Kerby, glaring at poor Mr. Good Citizen Wong Ding Yee.

They became aware of a twittering voice. The two old ladies they had run past were approaching.

"Scare a body out of her wits, rushing by like that!" one was saying indignantly, but the other was chuckling.

"Oh, now, Martha, boys will be boys," she said.

"Hmp!" The first old lady paused to squint narrowly at them. "And now what are you up to, young hoodlums? What are you doing?" she demanded in a very nosy way.

Preoccupied with the scene at the police station, Kerby gave the old ladies a flustered glance and blurted out an answer without thinking.

"We're watching my dog!"

"Well!" The nosy one reared her head back in an outraged way at this seemingly silly answer. Two boys peering into a dinky little box — watching their dog, indeed! But her friend laughed heartily.

"Must be a very small dog," she remarked.

"Of all the impudence!" fumed the nosy one and marched away in a huff, followed by her friend laughing harder than ever. Kerby was sorry to have sounded fresh, but there was no way to explain, and no time, either. Things were happening at the police station. The station house cat had appeared, and he was a huge, battle-scarred alley cat. As he strolled around the corner of a desk, he and Waldo saw each other. Waldo assumed his Xerxes stance, lowering his head and lunging forward as he began barking.

Up went the cat's back. He seemed to swell to double his original size, with every hair standing out like a spike as he let out a yowl and spit at Waldo.

Waldo had made an unfortunate mistake.

What Waldo failed to understand was that this was no Xerxes he was up against now. This was a real back-fence tiger. With another spit and another yowl that was fearful to see even without hearing it, the cat sprang sideways, circled Waldo in a flash, and bounded onto his back.

With what must have been an ear-splitting yelp of surprise and pain as the cat dug his claws in, Waldo almost jerked little Mr. Wong off his feet. He yanked the line out of his hand and began racing around the room, banging against furniture and upsetting wastebaskets, while policemen jumped up out of chairs and the little laundryman waved his arms wildly.

"Waldo! Get away!" cried Kerby.

"Run! The door's open!"

"Shake that cat off!"

The boys were so excited that Fenton almost dropped the beaker. It was lucky no one came walking along the street just then to see them.

Meanwhile Waldo was accomplishing things. Whether it was good fortune or intelligence does not matter, but either luck or quick thinking caused him to run under a chair. The chair provided a low bridge, and the cat did not see it coming until too late. Waldo kept going, but the cat stayed behind with a bump.

"Attaboy, Waldo! Now, run!" cried Kerby. "Run for the — Oh, darn! The picture's gone again!"

It was enough to drive a fellow crazy. Kerby wanted to shake the box, or bang it the way his father banged a radio when it wouldn't work. His father always admitted it didn't do the radio any good, but said it made *him* feel better.

"Well, come on!" said Fenton. "No use standing here — let's find the police station!"

At that moment a man walked up carrying a bundle of laundry. He looked annoyed to find the shop closed.

"Darn it all, where's that crazy Ding-a-Ling now?" he muttered.

The boys stared at him blankly, and Fenton could not help repeating, "Ding-a-Ling?"

The man glanced at them and then grinned.

"Oh, that's his nickname. I guess you're not from around here, huh, boys?"

"No, sir," said Kerby, still too surprised to say more.

"He'll be right back, sir," said Fenton. "Please, could you tell us where the police station is?"

"Why?" asked the surprised man. "What's happened?"

"Nothing, sir, we just want to know. Please!"

"Well, it's up on Kermit Avenue, one block over," he said, pointing, "but —"

"Thanks!" cried the boys, and raced away, leaving him with his mouth open.

As they skidded around the corner onto Kermit Avenue, they nearly bumped into a small Chinese.

"Oh! Hey, you've got a customer waiting, Ding-a-Ling!" cried Kerby, and they raced on, leaving *him* with his mouth open.

"Gee! Ding-a-Ling!" panted Fenton as they pounded along. "We guessed his very nickname!"

"There! There it is!" cried Kerby.

There ahead of them was the police station. It looked exactly the way it had in the beaker, except that now four policemen were standing out in front.

Two were staring up the street, obviously looking for Waldo. A third was holding a big groggy-looking black cat in his arms, while a fourth was carefully feeling the animal's head.

"Say, that's quite a bump!" they heard him say.

One of the policemen who had been staring down the street turned and shrugged.

"Well, the heck with it. I'll put out a call to all cars on that dog, and maybe one of the prowl cars will spot him."

Kerby's heart skipped a beat. Now Waldo was Wanted By The Police! As they walked past the station, they watched the policemen go inside. As soon as the last officer had disappeared, the boys broke into a run again.

"Waldo must have gone this way," muttered Fenton as they ran. "They were all looking this way."

"Yes, and we'd better find him soon!"

"Let's duck into an alley and take another look in the beaker! He can't be far away now!"

If they stopped on the sidewalk to look, they would attract too much attention. There were too many people walking along the busy avenue.

"Here's an alley!"

"Yes, but it's too dark. We won't be able to see."

"That's so. Well, come on, we'll go down the next side street."

Leaving the thoroughfare, they turned into a narrow side street. It was dingy, but its sidewalks were empty and there was at least enough light to see by. They opened the lid of the box and peered in, thinking hard.

Again a picture came into view quickly.

"There he is! Look, he's in a house!"

"Thank goodness!"

A plump lady with tight-curled hair and a fluffy dress was petting Waldo and talking to him, and the way she was talking you just knew she was talking baby-talk, even without hearing it. But at least she was being nice to him. While they watched, she filled a bowl with water and set it on the floor.

Waldo drank greedily. He had had a busy evening, and he was thirsty.

"Good! She looks all right," said Kerby happily. He felt they were near the end of their quest at last. Waldo could not be far away at all now. "He must be close! I'll bet that's why we're getting a picture fast again."

"I'll bet so, too, Kerby. Doesn't take as much juice, being close."

"Well, now all we have to do is figure out where she lives, and — "

"Hey, whatcha got there?"

They had been so absorbed in watching Waldo and his new friend that they had not even noticed the approach of three big, slouchy, tough-looking boys. The boys had slipped into the side street and were now standing around them in a ring with mean grins on their faces. One of them stuck out his hand greedily.

"Let's see whatcha got there!"

7

THE BOYS had chosen a bad street to be caught in. It was a street of business buildings — factories and lofts — and they were all closed. Except for themselves and the gang that had them surrounded, no one was in sight. There was no one to ask for help. Kerby and Fenton exchanged a swift sidewise glance, and Fenton held the box closer to him.

"It's nothing," he told the boys.

The gang leader looked at each of his friends and then snickered.

"Well, if it's nothing, then hand it over."

"No! You don't understand! It's nothing that —"

But the bully was impatient. He reached out and snatched at the box Fenton was trying to protect.

"Come on, give it here before I —"

As he tried to jerk it out of Fenton's hands, both of them lost hold of it. The box seemed to leap into the air.

"Stop!" cried Kerby, but it was too late. The box smashed to the pavement between them.

Crash! Broken glass tinkled.

POUF!

A round ball of smoke rolled up into the air, spinning as it came. Kerby and Fenton had seen such a ball of smoke before.

The other boys had not.

All their swagger vanished at once. Their fearless leader leaped backwards, fell over, hit his head, and scrambled up holding it with both hands.

"Yi! It's a bomb!" squealed one of the others. Bumping together and tripping over one another's feet in an effort to get away fast, the three fled down the street in a panic. After one glance of blank dismay at the shattered beaker, Kerby and Fenton instinctively raced away in the other direction, back toward Kermit Avenue.

They turned the corner and ran for a block before pulling up, panting, outside a large, busy, well-lighted furniture store. Then there was time to let their feelings catch up with them. Anger burned through Kerby.

"Those crumbs! I wish we'd been big enough to — to — Now they've fixed things good!"

Swiftly his red anger turned to black despair.

"We'll never find Waldo now," he predicted gloomily. A

crumpled paper cup was lying near the store entrance where someone had dropped it. Kerby kicked it into the gutter as hard as he could. He wished it were one of those boys. "Just when we were getting close, too!"

But Fenton was busy bouncing brain waves off the buildings. He stared fiercely into space.

"Think, Kerby! Think! When we were looking in the beaker that last time, did you notice anything that might give us a clue? Anything at all?"

Kerby sighed heavily. The effort seemed hopeless. But he dutifully knitted his brows and tried his best to remember every little detail of what he had seen.

Soon he shrugged.

"I can't remember a single thing that's any good," he grumbled. "All I remember is, there was a window behind them."

"Behind Waldo and that lady? That's right."

"It was light outside . . ."

"Yes. It didn't seem as light as this street, though."

"No, not quite."

"So maybe it looked out on a side street."

"Maybe. Oh, and another thing — the light was sort of flickering."

Fenton looked pleased.

"That's right, it was!"

"But why, I wonder? What kind of light flickers that way?"
They puzzled over this for a moment.

"Maybe there was a sign outside that was going on and off,"
Fenton suggested.

"Maybe so. But there's lots of signs that do that. Waldo
could be almost anywhere!"

"Well, not quite," said Fenton, thinking intently. "He
didn't have much of a head start on us. And when we looked
in the beaker he was already inside somebody's apartment. He
couldn't have run far in that time. He must either be somewhere along this street or not far down a side street. So let's
start looking for an electric sign going on and off."

They turned and gazed along the avenue they were on.
And as they did, they hardly knew whether to be encouraged
or discouraged. At first glance, it seemed as if half the signs
in sight were blinking on and off . . . ACME FURNITURE
MART . . . GEM PARKING . . . DELUXE LUNCH . . . CUT-RATE
DRUGS . . . CHOP SUEY . . .

"It could be any one of them!" groaned Kerby as they
walked slowly along, gawking up at the buildings.

Above most of the stores on both sides of the street there
were apartments. Was Waldo in one of them? And if so, how
on earth would they ever be able to tell which one? Looking

68

up at those shabby red brick walls and open windows, Kerby felt his heart sink even lower. Their search seemed hopeless now.

In many of the apartments, people were sitting with their heads out the windows, watching the crowds on the street and trying to get a breath of air. Kerby peered up anxiously, hoping that one of them would look like the woman they had seen with Waldo. But none of them did.

The boys came to a side street and gave it a close inspection both ways. They saw no signs going on and off.

"I don't see how he could have run much farther than this," declared Kerby. "Maybe we've already passed the place."

"Maybe. Well, let's keep going."

"That's about all we can do."

They plodded on to the next corner, craned their necks down the side street — and grabbed each other by the arm.

Partway down the block on the other side was a restaurant with a neon sign across the front of it. Some of the neon tubes were having trouble, the way such signs sometimes will.

The sign was flickering.

"That's it! *That's* the way it was, Fenton!"

"Yes! Come on!"

They hurried down the block and stopped across from the restaurant. Their first feeling of elation quickly drained away.

There were apartments above the restaurant, and across from it. Which of those many windows was the right one? Which was the one they had seen in the beaker?

"I don't know where to begin," Fenton confessed.

"Neither do I," said Kerby. But Waldo, he felt sure now, was somewhere in one of those buildings. They were getting close. They had to be! If they had to go inside each building and knock on every door until they found him, Kerby was ready to do it.

Several children were playing on the sidewalks, but luckily they were neither as big nor as mean-looking as those other boys Kerby and Fenton had had trouble with. Lots of grown-ups were outside on this street, too. Some were leaning against the iron railings in front of the basement entrances, and some were sitting on the steep front steps that ran up to parlor floor entrances. One old man had brought a wicker armchair out onto the landing at the top of one set of steps. He was sitting there in solid comfort, smoking a bulldog pipe. Here and there women were leaning out of windows, gossiping with friends outside, but none of them looked like the lady the boys were seeking.

"Say!"

Suddenly Fenton had brightened up. His eyes were sparkling with an idea.

70

"Listen, Kerby, Waldo certainly didn't walk inside one of these houses and scratch on somebody's door. That lady must have been walking along the street and seen him. Maybe by then he'd stopped running and was wondering what to do next. And he was still dragging that clothesline, so he would have been easy to catch, especially if it was someone who didn't scare him. That means she was probably outdoors on the street when she found him, and took him inside."

"Well? . . . Oh!"

Light dawned for Kerby. He smote his forehead and cried out happily.

"Sure! That means that anybody sitting outside must have noticed her bringing him home!"

"Right!"

"Well, come on, let's ask someone!"

They glanced around eagerly, wondering whom to try first.

"How about that old man sitting over there smoking his pipe? He looks as though he's been there for a long time."

"Let's go!"

A fringe of white hair surrounded the old man's pink bald head, and his eyebrows were white and bushy. He had a large lumpy nose and a squared-off sort of mouth. He gripped his pipe firmly with his teeth and puffed on it in a deliberate way, two puffs at a time. His thickset body filled the wicker armchair as he sat in it squarely with his feet planted squarely in front of him. When the boys came up the steps he cocked an eye sideways at them without moving his head.

"Excuse me, sir, but have you seen a lady come along with a small dog?" asked Fenton.

"A sort of flop-eared dog with brown eyes," Kerby added earnestly, forgetting that most dogs have brown eyes.

The old man stared at them with pale blue eyes and puffed twice on his pipe.

"Lady with a dog, you say?" He thought this over and puffed twice more. While he was doing so, a woman in a window nearby, who had overheard their question, put in her two cents' worth.

"There's no one in this building with a dog except Missus Nolan, and hers is one of them little Mexican things."

By now the old man had finished his puffing. He ignored the woman in the window entirely.

"Missus Kenwick come home with a dog," he told the boys.

"She did? When?" Kerby cried eagerly.

"While ago."

"Here?"

Puff, puff.

"Yes."

"Where is she? Where's she live?"

Puff, puff.

"Third floor front."

Leaving the old man in the middle of a puff, the boys rushed inside and up the shabby staircase.

"Third floor *front*," exulted Fenton. "Just right to see the sign flickering through the window!"

"Sure!" said Kerby, and his heart seemed to dance on ahead of him as he thought about Waldo, only a few steps away now. He was sure the lady would let him have Waldo, once she saw he was Kerby's own dog. She had looked nice.

On the third floor they found a door with a smudgy card over the doorbell. *Kenwick* was penciled on the card. Kerby hesitated, gathered his courage, and knocked.

Silence.

He knocked again. And again. But there was no response. None at all. Not a sound came from inside the apartment.

What was wrong? Was the lady keeping quiet? And was she making Waldo keep quiet, too?

Kerby decided he would soon put an end to that! If Waldo was inside, he would soon know it!

"Waldo!" he called.

They listened.

Not a sound.

The boys exchanged a look of blank and bitter disappointment. Then they turned without a word and hurried down the stairs.

8

THE OLD MAN'S blue eyes turned toward the boys as they burst out of the open door, but otherwise he did not move. He continued to puff placidly on his pipe.

"She's not there!" announced Kerby.

Puff, puff.

"I know she ain't," said the old man.

Puff, puff.

"I never said she was," he pointed out.

Puff, puff.

"You asked me where she lived, and I told you."

This time the old man took his pipe out of his mouth, examined its smoking bowl, tamped down the smouldering tobacco with a horny finger, and then set the pipe back in place between his teeth. The boys waited anxiously, but this time experience told them to be more patient.

After several puffs had gotten the pipe going again to his satisfaction, the old man went on.

"If you hadn't been in such an all-fired hurry, I'd have told you something else," he added with a disapproving grunt.

"Yes, sir," Kerby said meekly.

Puff, puff.

"I'd have told you she wasn't home because she went out again."

"With the dog?" cried Kerby, unable to restrain his eagerness.

The old man, after staring at him for a moment, nodded.

"Gee! Please, which way did she go?"

The old man jerked his head to one side.

"Thanks!" cried the boys, and started to leap down the steps — only to stop, both of them, at almost the same instant. They glanced at each other, turned back, and sheepishly mounted the steps again.

"Do you have any idea *where* she went, sir?" Kerby asked carefully.

The old man stared at him again. Then suddenly and unexpectedly he chuckled.

"That's more like it," he said. "Well, I'll tell you, boys. Missus Kenwick has a brother that runs a delicatessen on Burbank Avenue. I wouldn't be surprised if she wasn't going there. I suppose it'd be your dog she found, wouldn't it?"

"Yes, sir."

Puff, puff.

"Well, you go to the corner, turn left, and two blocks down you'll find Kratzmeyer's Delicatessen. Next to Galucci's Bakery."

"Thanks!"

This time the boys did not hesitate. They jumped down the steps and scampered up the street, certain at last that they had Waldo exactly located. Still, they had experienced so many disappointments that Kerby remained uneasy.

For one thing, why was Mrs. Kenwick taking Waldo to the delicatessen? Why hadn't she simply kept him at home in her apartment?

"We've got to be careful now," said Fenton, echoing his thoughts. "We'd better try to find out what's going on before we say anything. But we can't just walk in and hang around, either."

"I guess we'd better buy something."

"That's right. We can look around as if we're deciding what to buy."

Following the old man's directions, they turned onto Burbank Avenue. Soon they saw the delicatessen ahead of them on the other side of the street.

"There it is! Kratzmeyer's Delicatessen."

"With Galucci's Bakery next to it, like he said."

Kerby felt his heartbeat quicken at the sight. He struggled to hold down his excitement. Was Waldo truly just a few steps away this time?

Fenton gave him a tense glance.

"Try to act relaxed and casual."

"You look pretty wild yourself," retorted Kerby.

That made Fenton laugh, and helped them both.

"I'll bet I do at that. Here, let's stop a minute and simmer down."

They paused and made a special effort to smooth out their facial expressions and to stop breathing as if they had just run the hundred-yard dash. Kerby wished he had as good a poker face as Fenton. He would simply have to do his best.

"Ready?"

"Yes."

They walked into the delicatessen.

Behind a cluttered counter a small bald-headed man was fixing a hot pastrami sandwich for a customer. The small man was talking at a great rate while he worked.

"So that crazy sister of mine, what you think she did now? Found some stray dog in the street and brought it over to give my kids! Nothing doing, I says to her, we got enough troubles already without getting a dog too. I should pay good money for a dog license! And besides, right now they're out after stray dogs, rounding them up. So I told her nothing doing, and then I phoned the police station and told them I had this stray dog here. So that made her mad, and she went stamping out of here."

"What did the police say?"

"They're coming over."

The customer glanced around the small shop. He leaned forward to look behind the counter.

"Where is this mutt?"

Mr. Kratzmeyer jerked a thumb over his shoulder before slicing the sandwich.

"I got him tied up out in the back alley."

"Oh."

Mr. Kratzmeyer went on to say some more things about his crazy sister, and under cover of his remarks Kerby and Fenton, wild-eyed again, held a whispered consultation. With the police on the way, they were in real trouble. Now that Mr. Kratzmeyer had reported Waldo, he would certainly never let them take Waldo away before the police arrived. And if the boys had to try to explain everything to the police! . . . Well, once again Kerby saw visions of himself back in that psychiatrist's office!

"Order something, Fenton. Keep him busy while I get

Waldo," he muttered. He was desperate. "When I've got him I'll whistle."

"Okay. But remember, I'll have to wait for the sandwiches," Fenton mumbled in reply. "If I try to leave without paying for them, he'll come after me and then we'll all get caught for sure. You get going, and turn into the first side street you come to. I'll catch up as fast as I can."

Sometimes it is fortunate that grown-ups pay so little attention to children. Neither man took the slightest notice of the fact that one of the two boys who were waiting had slipped out of the store. Only when Mr. Kratzmeyer had finished making the hot pastrami sandwich and had put it on a plate did he look at Fenton and say, "What'll you have, sonny?"

Fenton had been studying the list of sandwiches. Egg salad was cheapest.

"Two eeee —"

He had to stop and clear his throat because his voice had squeaked so. He tried again.

"Two egg s-salad s-sandwiches, please."

"Two egg salad. To take out?"

"Y-yes, sir."

"White or rye?"

"Wh-white, p-p-p-pl —"

Then Fenton's voice forsook him entirely as his heart flew

into his throat. And what made this happen was the sound of excited barking that suddenly began out in back of the store — and almost as suddenly stopped.

"That's the mutt now," Mr. Kratzmeyer remarked to the man with the hot pastrami sandwich, who had sat down at a little table. "What kind of bread did you say, sonny?"

"Wh-white," squeaked Fenton.

"White." Mr. Kratzmeyer nodded. "You got quite a stutter, huh? I got a nephew who had a terrible stutter till he was almost twenty years old, *terrible* stutter. Then one day it cleared up just like that," he declared, pausing in the midst of laying out slices of bread to snap his fingers. "Just like that. Maybe it'll happen to you, too."

Fenton nodded, too scared to try to say anything. Mr. Kratzmeyer's experienced hands were moving with a swiftness worthy of a magician's as he fixed the sandwiches.

"Soon's I finish here I'll go see what that mutt was barking about," he remarked to the man with the hot pastrami.

Fenton caught his breath. He had to delay Mr. Kratzmeyer at all costs! At all costs, that is, up to eighty cents. That was all the money he had left after paying the bus fares.

"H-how m-much are p-p-pickles?" he blurted.

"Which kind?"

"Well, let's s-s-see . . ."

Fenton took a good long look at all the different kinds in the showcase. Mr. Kratzmeyer waited for him to decide. Fenton took as much time deciding as he dared, and while he pretended to study the pickles he was thinking hard. Normally, of course, he did not stutter, but since Mr. Kratzmeyer thought he did, he would make the most of it. After all, stuttering took time.

"W-w-well," he said painfully, "h-h-h-how much are th-th-those, p-p-p-please?"

The entrance to the alley was alongside the delicatessen. After a swift glance around to make sure nobody was watching him, Kerby darted into it.

It was dark in the alley, but not pitch dark. The back door of the delicatessen and a side door opening into the bakery each threw a rectangle of light out on the garbage cans, the used cartons and other rubbish that lined the blank walls. It was a blind alley. That is to say, it did not go on through to the next street, but ended behind the delicatessen.

For an instant, as he rounded the corner of the building, Kerby almost forgot his fears and his worries and everything else in the joy of seeing Waldo lift his head eagerly off his paws. Waldo was tied to a rusty pipe that ran up the side of the building. He had been crouched down, unhappy and forlorn, shivering with misery. Now he sprang to his feet and began barking a joyous greeting before Kerby could leap on him and make him stop.

"Quiet! Ssh!" Kerby threw one arm around his wriggling friend and grabbed his jaws with the other. Fortunately, in leaping forward to greet Kerby, Waldo had cut his own barking short by nearly strangling himself with the line around his neck. And being a very smart dog when it came to understanding orders, even though he did not always feel like obeying them, Waldo immediately got the idea when Kerby whispered to him. He stopped barking at once. He subsided into low whimpers of delight, and even stopped those when Kerby shushed him again. From then on he concentrated on tail-wagging and hand-licking, neither of which made much noise.

As soon as he knew Waldo would be quiet, Kerby went to work to untie the line. But the knot was a hard one, and he got nowhere. He thought bitterly of the jackknife at home on his desk. Why had he not thought to put it in his pocket?

"Hold still, Waldo!" he whispered, and struggled on. And as usual with knots, just when he thought the struggle was hopeless, the knot gave a tiny bit. Another minute, and he had worked it loose. With a shiver of relief that went through him like electricity, he freed the line from the pipe.

"Come on!" he said, and started cautiously back around the rear corner of the delicatessen building.

He had no more than stepped into the alley when he leaped back again and yanked Waldo with him.

A police car had just pulled up out in front. He had seen it slide slowly by, coming to a stop.

In another few seconds a policeman would be inside the store talking to Mr. Kratzmeyer, and Mr. Kratzmeyer would bring him out to get Waldo. Yet there was no chance to run out of the alley, because the police car was standing right there, and the driver would still be in the car.

They were trapped. Trapped in a blind alley!

9

"ANYTHING else?" asked Mr. Kratzmeyer.

Tensely, Fenton was doing his arithmetic. The sandwiches were thirty cents apiece. That was sixty. The pickle he had chosen was ten. That made seventy.

"W-w-well," he said, while Mr. Kratzmeyer waited — and he was waiting now with growing impatience, "how m-much are th-those n-n-next p-p-pickles?"

"These?"

"N-no, th-th —"

"These?"

"Y-yes."

"Ten cents too."

"Two for t-ten cents?"

"No, no, ten cents apiece! Look, sonny, make up your mind!"

"Th-those, then."

"How many?"

"One."

Sighing loudly, Mr. Kratzmeyer fished out a large sour pickle to add to the dill pickle Fenton had already chosen.

"Okay, that'll be eighty cents in all."

Fenton fished out his money and managed to drop a dime on the floor. But would that dime roll into some nice corner where it would be hard to recover, where it would take time to find? No. It bounced once and stopped in the middle of the floor.

But at that instant his agony of stalling ended. Something worse took its place. A police car pulled up out in front. Fenton looked up from retrieving his dime to see a policeman climbing out.

Automatically, moving like a zombie, Fenton put his money on the counter and accepted his bag of sandwiches and pickles. One look at that policeman, and he felt as though he had been dipped in a quick-freeze vat.

"Hi, Max," said the policeman as he strode inside. "Where's this dog you got?"

"Well! Hi, Joe," said Mr. Kratzmeyer. "He's out in back."

"He sounds like the dog a Chinese laundryman brought to the station that tore things up and got away. I want to see him."

"See him? Ain't you going to take him?"

The policeman drew himself up grandly. He was insulted by this suggestion.

"What do you mean, take him? Listen, I'm no dogcatcher. We called the dog pound. They're sending over a truck to pick him up. I just want to have a look at him."

"Okay, so come have a look," said Mr. Kratzmeyer, shrugging.

He led the way back through the small stockroom that was behind the front part of the store. Deciding he was curious, too, the hot pastrami man followed them, and Fenton tagged along behind him on legs that had no feeling left in them at all.

Mr. Kratzmeyer opened the back screen door and stepped outside.

"Here he is . . ."

He stopped, amazed. Because he found he was pointing at empty air.

The dog was gone. He had disappeared without a trace.

"Hey! Somebody stole him!" cried Mr. Kratzmeyer.

The policeman eyed him sharply.

"How's that again?"

"I say, someone stole him! He was right here!" insisted Mr. Kratzmeyer, grabbing hold of the iron pipe and pointing dramatically at the ground. "I tied him up myself."

90

"You must not have tied him up very good," observed the policeman.

"Listen, I know how to tie a knot!" yelled Mr. Kratzmeyer. He stamped his feet, he was so insulted. "I tell you, somebody stole him!"

"Okay, okay," said the policeman, grinning.

Then his eyes lighted up. He stepped forward, leaned down, and picked up a crumpled piece of paper.

"Hey, this is my lucky day." He held it up. "Look what I found. A dollar bill!"

Mr. Kratzmeyer's face fell.

"I must have thrown it out with the trash!" he said, eyeing it longingly.

"Finders keepers," said Joe the policeman. "Tell you what, Max — I'll spend it in your place. Fix Tim and me a couple of hot pastramis."

A philosopher when he had to be, Mr. Kratzmeyer shrugged once more.

"Okay, fair enough."

They all went inside again, speculating on who could have taken the dog, and who would have wanted a mutt like that in the first place. All but Fenton, that is. Fenton stayed where he was, standing unobtrusively against the wall.

When they were gone, he stepped forward, staring around

him and applying logic to the situation. Kerby had gone into the alley. He had not whistled to signal that he was coming out of it. Therefore he must still be in it.

Quietly, cautiously, Fenton called in a low voice.

"Psst! Kerby!"

In the far corner, among the cartons Mr. Kratzmeyer and the bakery had thrown away, there was a large one marked *Paper Napkins, One Gross*. Now the top of it began to move. Kerby's head appeared like that of some frightened jack-in-the-box.

Fenton rushed over, his eyes bright with keen appreciation of Kerby's brain waves. But there was no time to spare for compliments and congratulations.

"Kerby! Is Waldo in there with you?"

"Yes! Down, boy!" ordered Kerby, as Waldo stood up in the box to welcome Fenton. "But what do we do now?"

The sound of another car pulling up at the head of the alley caught their attention. The police car was parked in front of the delicatessen, on one side of the alley entrance. Now a truck had pulled up and stopped on the other side of it. With sudden understanding, Fenton guessed what it was.

"That's the dogcatcher's truck!"

Kerby gasped.

"We've got to get out of here quick!" said Fenton.

"Yes, but how?"

Fenton's eyes darted around in every direction, seeking an answer to this seemingly hopeless question. Another carton over near the bakery door caught his eye. He hurried to it.

It was a fancy white carton about two feet square, and it had a smear of rosebud frosting on it.

On its side, printed with a black marking pencil, were the words *Wedding Cake — Handle with Care.*

Thoughtfully, Fenton bent down, scraped off the frosting with one finger, and flicked it away.

"Hey, Kerby," he said softly.

Fifteen seconds later Kerby and Fenton walked out of the alley.

Kerby was carrying the white carton, and Fenton was fussing along beside him.

"Be careful, now!" he cried. "Just mess up that frosting, and see what Sis will say!"

"Okay, okay! I'm being careful!" snapped Kerby.

With a huge effort of will, he was keeping his eyes on the carton he was carrying and resisting the temptation to look either at the police car or the dogcatcher's truck.

"Whatever you do, don't look at them," Fenton had said. "Act as if we don't even know they're there."

But Fenton himself was having trouble. He could feel the eyes of the police car driver on them as if those eyes had been twin flame throwers. Yet actually the policeman was merely looking at the boys with lazy amusement.

"Don't drop it!" he called, with a chuckle.

Fenton smiled at him wildly.

"We won't!" he replied, and hurried Kerby on down the street. Not that Kerby needed hurrying. Heavy as the box was, it was all he could do not to break into a run. He felt as though at any second Mr. Kratzmeyer or Joe the policeman or the dogcatcher or the hot pastrami man would come out and see them and say, "Hey! Where are you kids going with that box?"

But no such dreaded words came their way. In another moment they were turning the corner.

Kerby drew a deep breath.

"Take it easy, boy!" he murmured to the box. They had poked some air holes in the back. He whispered through those. "Just take it easy . . . Now, where can we get a taxicab, Fenton?"

Fenton made a strange noise in his throat.

"Kerby," he said in a bleak voice.

"What?"

"I noticed you put Waldo's collar on him. When did you do that?"

"Well, I thought it might help to have it on him if the policeman found us. It would prove right away that he had a new license, the way he's supposed to. So just before I climbed into the box with him I pulled his collar out of my pocket. And before any of you came outside, I had put it on him," Kerby explained proudly.

He felt he had been pretty clever to think of doing that. But Fenton's next few words changed his feelings.

"I thought so," said Fenton. "Kerby, I hate to tell you, but . . . Listen, let me carry the box for a minute."

"Why? I'm doing okay."

"Give it here."

"Well, all right, but . . ."

"Here, you take the sandwich bag."

They exchanged the box and the bag.

"Now," said Fenton. "Feel in your pocket and see if you've still got that dollar you had."

"What? Why, of course I have . . ."

A horrible shock zigzagged down Kerby's spine.

"It's gone!"

Fenton nodded mournfully.

"When you jerked the collar out of your pocket, you must

have jerked the bill out with it. That policeman found it."

Kerby's shoulders slumped.

"Oh, boy! Now what'll we do?"

How on earth would they get home?

"I don't know, Kerby," admitted Fenton.

"Do you think we can sneak Waldo home on a bus?"

Sadly Fenton glanced at the bag Kerby was carrying and shook his head.

"No. We haven't even got bus fare. I spent every cent I had on sandwiches and pickles."

Kerby sagged some more. He felt like a mechanical toy that after being tightly wound up for a long time had finally run down and could go no further. The boys stopped and faced each other, feeling utterly defeated.

"Gee, to get this far and then be stuck!" groaned Kerby. He looked up and down the street. "If only someone we knew would come along and give us a ride!"

"Fat chance of that!" said Fenton bitterly. "Besides, there's no one we know that wouldn't tell our families, if they picked us up downtown like this. And with Waldo in a wedding cake box, for Pete's sake!"

All was lost. Kerby knew Fenton was right. All he had to do was think of several different friends of his family. He knew what would happen if any of them came along and picked them up. They would ask a million questions. They would be sure to call up his family in the morning to tell them about it and ask *them* a lot of questions, too. There was nobody he could think of who would help them out now without telling on them.

An old car came clattering down the street with such a rattle-bang that it made him look around. He turned away to look at Fenton again and worry some more — and then his head whirled back in the direction of the approaching car.

With a wild cry, Kerby flung up his arm.

"Mrs. Graymalkin!" he shouted. "Help!"

10

THE ANCIENT SEDAN swung in to the curb and shuddered to a stop. Her bright old eyes snapping, Mrs. Graymalkin flashed her familiar gap-toothed smile at Kerby. But her tone of voice was brisk and businesslike.

"Hop in quickly before that police car turns the corner."

The order was hardly necessary. Kerby had yanked the door open in a flash. And Fenton, after a single astounded glance at Mrs. Graymalkin, had all but dived in head first with the box. Kerby scrambled in behind him and shut the door.

"On the floor and keep your heads down," ordered Mrs. Graymalkin. She was promptly obeyed. "Here they come," she warned.

The boys held their breath. They could hear the police car purring alongside them.

". . . and there they go," she added, with a pleased cackle. "Now! Now to get you home."

The car began to rattle and bump as it moved forwar again.

"Stay down for another block or two, and then we'll be safe. Is Waldo all right?" she asked calmly, as though it were the most natural thing in the world for boys to walk around with a dog in a wedding cake box. And how did she know he was in it, anyway? Kerby felt his spine prickle as he wondered about this strange matter. What was she doing here? She was the one person he knew in the whole wide world who would never give them away — and she had suddenly appeared! Was Fenton wrong? Was she . . . ?

"Waldo's fine, thank you, but I think he'd like to be let out of the box," Kerby replied to her question.

"In a minute, in a minute," said Mrs. Graymalkin.

Obediently the boys left the box closed and kept their own heads down. They murmured words of comfort and reassurance to Waldo. Waldo had been very good. He had not whined or whimpered once, even though it was surely no fun to be cooped up in a box for so long.

As the car jounced onward, Kerby and Fenton glanced at each other. The expression on Fenton's face as they crouched together on the floor of the car did not need any words to explain it. Kerby could see that Fenton had found this the most thrilling experience of all. At last he had actually seen

Mrs. Graymalkin for himself! At last he could talk to her, too! He was obviously impressed, deeply impressed.

"All right, boys," said Mrs. Graymalkin. "We should be all right now. You can let Waldo out, but I'd keep him on the floor just to be on the safe side."

They sat up on the seat and took the lid off the box. The next few moments were devoted to ecstatic whines, frantic tail-wagging, and wild tongue-lapping. When Waldo felt he had suitably expressed his pleasure at being back with the boys again, and was willing to sit down on the floor between them, Mrs. Graymalkin resumed the conversation.

"Well, Fenton, it's nice to meet you. Kerby has told me so much about you."

Offhand Kerby could not recall having told her very much about Fenton, but he let that pass.

"It's an honor to meet you, Mrs. Graymalkin," said Fenton with deep feeling. He still looked almost stunned with amazement, and as Kerby eyed his friend, Fenton leaned forward slightly, studying Mrs. Graymalkin with quick, keen glances. And suddenly, just as though he could read his friend's mind, Kerby knew that Fenton was dying to ask her a question, but could not get up nerve enough to do it. Furthermore, Kerby knew what the question was — so he asked it himself.

"Mrs. Graymalkin," he said, "how on earth did you ever happen to come along just when we needed help?"

The old lady gave one of those barnyard imitations that served her for a laugh. She sounded just like a happy chicken.

"Why, that's simple enough, Kerby," she said, and even though he could not see her face he could well imagine how her eyes were twinkling. "After I met you in the park, I was so curious to know whether you would find Waldo that I decided to go get my old car out and see where you went. I saw you leave the house and take a bus, so I followed the bus until you got off. I saw you go to the laundry, and then to the police station — and oh, wasn't it a shame when those nasty boys made you drop the beaker? But you were very clever, the way you kept right on and figured out where Waldo was. I watched you stop at that house where the man was having a smoke, and I followed you when you went on to that delicatessen. When you came out of the alley carrying that box, I knew Waldo must be in it. Naturally I knew then that if you were going to get away perhaps I had better help."

The boys had perched on the edges of their seats listening, enthralled. Now Kerby sat back with a happy sigh.

"Gee, you sure did!" he said gratefully. "You really saved our necks!"

"Well, I'm so glad I could. And I enjoyed every minute of

it. It's just the sort of thing I love to do," said Mrs. Graymalkin with a titter. "I've often thought I would have liked to be a detective."

"Well, you certainly would make a good one!" Kerby declared with complete sincerity, though at the same time the thought of "Mrs. Graymalkin, Private Eye" almost made him laugh out loud. He glanced at Fenton again. Now that she had explained everything so logically, he was sure Fenton had regained completely his old faith in science. But Kerby was equally sure that Fenton's beliefs had been severely tested for a few minutes there.

Mrs. Graymalkin's old car might rattle and shake, but it moved right along. Now that they could relax enough to realize how hungry they were, the boys remembered the sandwiches. They offered Mrs. Graymalkin one, but when she assured them she was not hungry, they wolfed them down, sharing them with Waldo, of course. Fortunately Waldo did not care for any pickle, so they were able to split the pickles two ways. And by the time they had finished eating, they were almost home.

"Leave the cake box," said Mrs. Graymalkin. "I'll get rid of it for you."

"Thanks very much," said Kerby. "And thanks for everything!"

"Yes, and thanks for telling us how to make the beaker work," added Fenton. "That was really a scientific wonder!"

"Did you like it?" said Mrs. Graymalkin casually, as though it were hardly more than an interesting gadget. She tittered again. "I don't really know how those things work, but they *are* interesting, to be sure. Well, here we are! Quick, now, jump out and run in before anyone sees you!"

"Gosh, yes, we've got to put away the chemistry set!" cried Kerby, suddenly remembering. "We left it spread out all over the place!"

"Then away, away, away!" Mrs. Graymalkin cried merrily in her strange talking-crow voice, and they tumbled out of the car one after the other. Kerby shut the car door and turned to thank her again, but the old sedan was already grinding off with a growl of gears at a surprising speed. They had to be content to wave, and to see a bony old arm thrust out the window and a spidery old hand waved in farewall. At the same instant, lightning flashed overhead, flashed and crackled. The rickety old car turned a corner to the accompaniment of a drum-roll of thunder, and was gone.

"Gosh!" murmured Fenton. Then he shook himself, as though shaking off a spell. "Well, come on — we've got to move! I forgot all about the weather, but I can tell you it's going to storm any minute now. And that means your mother might show up, so let's go!"

Less than five minutes later they had every bit of the chemistry set assembled and put away. Waldo trotted around the basement sniffing everything, delighted to be home. When the boys had hidden it in its old place in the toy chest, they looked at each other thoughtfully. Kerby's eyes began to twinkle.

"Listen, Fenton. When Mrs. Graymalkin first showed up, didn't you wonder about her a little bit?"

Fenton's face turned red. He looked downright annoyed. But at the same time he was too honest not to admit the truth.

"Oh, all right!" he grumbled. "Maybe I did, for a minute there . . . But do you know what I really think about her now, Kerby?" Fenton pointed his finger for emphasis. "I think Mrs. Graymalkin is secretly one of the greatest scientists in the world!"

Kerby's mouth fell open.

"I mean it, Kerby! Listen, didn't you notice how she seemed to know every little thing we did? All right! How could she have seen everything she told about by just following us in her car? Well, let me just tell you something. You couldn't see the dashboard of her car from where you were sitting, because you were behind her. But I could. You know the place on the

106

dashboard panel where most cars have a radio? Well, Mrs. Graymalkin didn't have any radio there. Instead, she had a round, shiny hole in it. And that hole looked exactly like our beaker did!"

As Fenton spoke, a loud crackle of lightning made them jump. A tremendous bang of thunder shook the house. A few drops of rain spattered against the basement windows, and then the skies opened. Rain came down in torrents.

"Gosh! We better go up and close windows!" cried Kerby. They all raced up the basement steps.

While they were closing windows, the telephone rang. Kerby answered.

"Well!" said Mr. Maxwell, sounding both pleased with Kerby and pleased with himself. "Your mother wanted to run home and see if you were all right, but I told her you boys had sense enough to come in out of the rain. I'm glad to find I was right!"

"We've just been closing the windows," Kerby told him virtuously.

"Good for you! And did you get Waldo's dog tag put on all right?"

"Yes, Pop."

"That's my boy. Well, as long as you're inside, we won't hurry home."

"I should say not, Pop. Take your time."

"Waldo inside too?"

"Oh, sure!"

"Fine. Your mother says to tell you if you want a late snack, there's plenty of stuff in the icebox."

"Great!" said Kerby fervently.

When he had hung up, he turned to Fenton and Waldo and grinned.

"Mom says we can have a late snack if we want it."

"Wow!"

Fenton closed his eyes, licked his lips, and smiled blissfully.

"Well, let's not let it get any later!" he cried.

As for Waldo, he was already sitting in front of the icebox!